The Monkey King

Retold by Rosie Dickins

Illustrated by Germano Ovani

Based on a translation by Evelyn Ong

Reading consultant: Alison Kelly,
Roehampton University

Contents

Chapter 1

Monkey goes to Heaven

Bring me bananas!

Monkey was the cleverest animal in China. He was the king of the monkeys, but he was not a good king. He was always stealing food and demanding presents.

In fact, Monkey caused so much trouble that people prayed to Heaven for help.

The Emperor of Heaven heard them. "Mischievous Monkey!" he cried. "What shall we do?"

"I know," said the Empress. "Let's give him a job in Heaven where we can keep an eye on him."

Now, the Emperor needed a new groom to look after his horses, so he agreed.

Monkey was very proud to be called to Heaven. And he loved looking after the heavenly horses, with their bright coats and gleaming hooves.

One day, Monkey was
chatting to a footman. "Of
course, my job is much more
important than yours," he
boasted.

"You? You're just a groom," scoffed the footman. "You're not important."

"But I'm the Great Monkey King!" Monkey snapped. "I deserve better." And he stormed out of Heaven.

The Emperor shook his fist when he heard the news. "My soldiers will fetch him back."

But the Empress tugged his sleeve. "Why don't we give him a better job?" she said.

Then he'll come back without a fight.

So the Emperor sent a messenger to tell Monkey he had been promoted.

"You are now Keeper of the Heavenly Peach Garden," said the messenger, bowing.

"It's a very important job,"
continued the messenger.
"These are magic peaches!"
    "Magic, huh?" said Monkey
thoughtfully. "OK, I accept."

So Monkey found himself
strolling around the Peach
Garden with two gardeners.
First, they showed him trees
full of small yellow peaches.

"The yellow peaches ripen every three thousand years," said the first gardener. "Eating them makes you wise and clever."

In the middle, Monkey saw trees covered with orange fruit.

"The orange peaches ripen every six thousand years," said the second gardener. "They help you to fly."

At the back of the garden was a row of very old trees. Here and there hung a heavy purple peach.

"The purple peaches take nine thousand years to ripen," said the gardeners. "Eating one makes you live forever."

This is even better!

Monkey was thrilled to be in charge of such important trees. He spent hours in the garden, bossing the gardeners around.

One day, he spotted a ripe purple peach, high in the leaves. "They won't miss just one," he told himself. And he climbed through the branches and gobbled it up.

Mmm, delicious!

It tasted so good, he did the same thing the next time he saw a ripe purple peach...

and the next...

and the next.

Chapter 2
The Peach Banquet

As summer drew to a close, the Empress of Heaven began to prepare for her yearly Peach Banquet.

19

First, the Empress sent
invitations to all the most
important gods.

Then, she told the cook to
prepare his finest dishes.

Cooking
with
peaches

And lastly, she sent the
Heavenly Fairies to pick the
magic peaches.

20

The Fairies picked a few yellow and orange peaches. But on the oldest trees, they found only broken twigs and torn leaves.

After a long search, they
spotted a single purple peach.
The branch bent as they
tugged at it, then snapped
back with a loud twang...

There was a yelp – and
Monkey appeared, rubbing
his nose. "Hey!" he shouted.
"That's MY peach!"

23

"The Empress needs it for her Peach Banquet," said the Fairies politely.

"A banquet? Where's my invitation?" screeched Monkey.

How dare she leave me out!

Furious, Monkey
cast a spell and froze
the Fairies to the spot.
Then he stormed off to
complain to the Empress.

As Monkey passed the banquet hall, he saw servants laying out food – spiced buns, sizzling meats, stir-fried vegetables and steaming rice...

Monkey sniffed the air hungrily. When no one was looking, he snatched a plate and ducked into a cupboard.

Inside, rows of bottles lined
the shelves. Monkey picked
one up and read the label.

MAGIC
POTION
gives
eternal life

He took a swig. It tasted
like honey and peaches.

"Yum! Just the thing to wash down my dinner," he thought. "I wonder if the other bottles taste as good?" And, one by one, he drank them all.

Suddenly, he heard voices. Servants were coming to fetch the bottles!

"The Empress is very upset about the missing peaches," said a voice. "It's lucky we have the potion to serve at the banquet instead..."

30

"Uh-oh," thought Monkey,
looking at the empty bottles.
"Time to get out of here..."

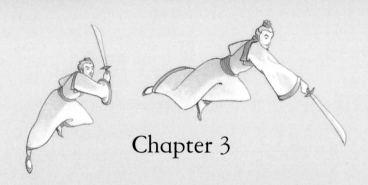

Chapter 3

Buddha's challenge

The Empress sighed. "The banquet is ruined," she said.

"It's all that Monkey's fault," thundered the Emperor. "I'll send my soldiers after him!"

But Monkey was a good
fighter, and the peaches and
potions had made him
impossible to kill. Every time
a soldier knocked him down,
he sprang up again unharmed.

"What shall we do?" cried the soldiers. "He's too strong!"

The Emperor frowned and pulled his beard.

"Let's ask Buddha to help," whispered the Empress.

Buddha was the most
powerful lord in Heaven.
He walked fearlessly into
Monkey's latest fight.

Monkey spun around.
"What do you want?"
he snapped rudely.

"I want you to behave yourself," said Buddha.

You don't know the trouble you've caused!

"Why should I listen to you?" retorted Monkey. "I am the Great Monkey King. *I* should be Emperor of Heaven!"

Buddha laughed. "What makes you so special?"

"I'm a great fighter, I will live forever and I can leap thousands of miles in one go," Monkey said proudly.

Smiling, Buddha stretched
out his hand. "If you can leap
further than my hand, I will
make you Emperor of Heaven,"
he said. "But if you fail, you
must accept your punishment."

Buddha's hand looked no
bigger than a lotus leaf.

"Easy," scoffed Monkey. "Can
you really make me Emperor?"

"Of course," Buddha replied.
"Can you leap this far?"

39

In answer, Monkey took a huge leap. He whizzed through the air...

and finally landed beside five tall, pink pillars.

"The pillars at the end of
the world," he chuckled. "I've
won! But I'd better leave my
mark here, in case Buddha
tries to cheat."

Monkey plucked a hair from his head and whispered a magic word. The hair turned into a brush. Quickly, he painted a message...

Before he left, he piddled on the pillars as well.

When he got back, Buddha
was standing on the same spot.
"Silly Monkey," he said.
"You were in my hand
all the time!"

"You're wrong," replied
Monkey. "I got to the end of
the world and I wrote my
name on one of the pillars."

43

"Look at my hand," said
Buddha sternly.
Monkey looked.

There on Buddha's finger
was a familiar message – and
there was a funny smell.

"B-but that's impossible!"
Monkey whimpered. "I wrote
on the pillars..." His voice
trailed off. The pillars *had*
looked like giant fingers.

"Time for a quick exit," he
decided, getting ready for
another leap.

But Buddha was even
quicker. At his command,
thunder roared and rocks
rained down, burying
Monkey under a
huge mountain.

The rocks didn't harm Monkey – the peaches and potions had made him too strong. But he couldn't move either.

"And there you will stay," Buddha declared, "until you are ready to mend your ways."

The Monkey King is a traditional Chinese tale. It was first written down nearly five hundred years ago, but people have been telling it for much longer. Today, Monkey is China's most popular superhero, appearing in books, cartoons, puppet shows and operas.

Series editor: Lesley Sims
Designed by Katarina Dragoslavic

First published in 2007 by Usborne Publishing Ltd., Usborne House, 83-85 Saffron Hill, London EC1N 8RT, England. www.usborne.com
Copyright © 2007 Usborne Publishing Ltd.